The Nutcracker

The Classic Edition

by E.T.A. Hoffmann

✳

Illustrated by Christina Hess

Kennebunkport, Maine

Dedicated to my mom and dad
Thank you for all your love and support

Table of Contents

Editor's Note

First published in 1816, E.T.A. Hoffmann's "The Nutcracker and the Mouse King" includes many elements ignored in Pyotr Ilyich Tchaikovsky's famous ballet adaptation, which was more closely inspired by a watered-down reworking of the story in 1844 by French author Alexandre Dumas, père. While many of the ballet's changes are cosmetic, such as renaming the protagonist from Marie to Clara, giving the adults different professions, and making the Nutcracker a gift for Clara alone rather than the whole family, several are more significant.

Hoffmann's original tale includes a pivotal story-within-a-story that explains how the Nutcracker became enchanted and why he is at odds with the Mouse King, as well as a second thrilling battle between the hero and his rodent nemesis that is missing from the ballet. While the ballet's Clara is mostly passive, Hoffman's Marie actively devises a plan for defeating the Mouse King and effects the transformation of her beloved toy into his human form through her ability to see through outward appearances. Perhaps the most striking difference in the two plots is the resolution; while the ballet traditionally ends with the young girl waking from a wondrous dream, Hoffman's story concludes with Marie and her now-human prince living happily ever after in the fantasy realm, though whether that should be taken in a literal or figurative sense is left to the reader's interpretation.

This heirloom edition of the Nutcracker story is abridged and lightly adapted from the 1886 Major Alex. Ewing translation, which was the first complete English-language translation directly from the original German and hews very close to the author's original wording and intentions.

Christmas Eve

On the 24th of December, Dr. Stahlbaum's children Fritz and Marie were not allowed to go into the best drawing room for any reason. Fritz, whispering in a mysterious fashion, confided to his young sister that he had heard rattlings and rustlings all day inside the forbidden rooms, as well as distant hammerings. Further, that a short time ago a man had gone creeping across the floor with a big box under his arm, though he was well aware that this man was Godpapa Drosselmeier.

Godpapa Drosselmeier had a black patch where his right eye ought to have been, and a fine white wig. He was a very clever man who knew all about clocks and watches. When one of the beautiful clocks in Dr. Stahlbaum's house was out of sorts and couldn't sing, Godpapa Drosselmeier would come, take off his wig and his yellow coat, tie on a blue apron, and proceed to stick sharp-pointed instruments into the inside of the clock until it came to life again and began to whirr and sing and strike as merrily as ever.

Whenever he came he always brought something delightful in his pockets for the children—perhaps a little man, who would roll his eyes and bow; or a box, out of which a little bird would jump. But for Christmas he always had some especially charming piece of ingenuity that was always taken and put away for safekeeping by the children's parents.

"Oh, what has Godpapa Drosselmeier made for us *this* time?" Marie cried, clapping her little hands.

Then the door to the drawing room opened, and Papa and Mama invited the children in. The two children stood speechless, with brilliant glances fixed on all the beautiful things. After a little, Marie cried, "Oh, how lovely! How lovely!" and Fritz gave several jumps of delight. The children had certainly been very well behaved all year to be thus rewarded; for never before had so many beautiful and delightful things been provided for them.

The great Christmas tree on the table bore many apples of silver and gold, and all its branches were heavy with sugar almonds, bonbons, and charming things to eat. All round the tree, everything shone and glittered in the loveliest manner. Oh, how many beautiful things there were!

Marie gazed at the most delightful dolls, and all kinds of toys. A little silk dress with many-tinted ribbons was hanging so she could admire it, which she did, crying out several times, "Oh, the lovely, darling little dress!"

Fritz, in the meantime, said that his new fox seemed a wildish sort of brute; but, no matter, he felt sure he would soon get him well in order. And he mustered his new squadron of hussars in red and gold uniforms, with real silver swords and mounted on shining white horses.

When the children had calmed down a little and were beginning upon the beautiful picture books, a tinkling bell announced the display of Godpapa Drosselmeier's Christmas present, which was concealed by a curtain. When this curtain was drawn, what did the children behold?

On a green lawn bright with flowers stood
a lordly castle with a great many shining windows
and golden towers. A chime of bells was going
on inside it; doors and windows opened, and very
small ladies and gentlemen walked up and down in the
rooms of it. In the central hall, little candles burned
in silver chandeliers; children in short
doublets danced to the chimes of the
bells. A gentleman in an emerald green

14

cloak came to a window, waved, and then disappeared inside again; even a tiny Godpapa Drosselmeier came now and then and stood at the castle door, then went in again.

After a short time, Fritz cried impatiently, "Godpapa Drosselmeier, please come out at that other door!"

"That can't be done, dear Fritz," answered Drosselmeier.

"Well," resumed Fritz, "make that green man walk about with the others. Or make the children come down," said Fritz. "I want to see them nearer."

"Nonsense, nothing of that sort can be done," cried Drosselmeier, with impatience. "The machinery must work as it's doing now; it can't be altered."

"It can't be done?" said Fritz. "Very well, if your little creatures in the castle can only do one thing, they're not worth much! No, give me my hussars. They move where I want them, and are not fastened up in a house."

Fritz moved to the other table, and sent his silver horses wheeling and charging right and left to his heart's content. Marie had slipped away softly too, for she was tired of the dancing of the puppets in the castle, though she did not like to show it as her brother did.

The Nutcracker

Marie was hesitant to come away from the table where the Christmas presents were laid out because she had just noticed something that she had not observed at first. In front of the tree she saw a most delightful little man who was standing quietly, as if waiting patiently to be noticed. His body was too tall and stout for his legs, and his head was a good deal too large. He had on a very pretty scarlet hussar's jacket with knobs and braiding, tan pantaloons, and the loveliest little boots. A short cloak made of wood sat on his shoulders and on his head was a matching crown.

As Marie kept looking at this little man, whom she had quite fallen in love with at first sight, she saw more and more clearly the sweet nature visible in his face. His green eyes beamed with kindliness. His chin was set off with a well-kept beard of brown cotton that drew attention to the sweet smile expressed by his bright red lips.

"Papa," cried Marie at last, "whose is that most darling little man beside the tree?"

"Well," was the answer, "that little fellow is going to crack nuts for all of you, and he is to belong to your sister Louise just as much as to you and Fritz."

Papa picked him up and lifted the end of his wooden cloak, causing the little man to open his mouth wider and wider, displaying two rows of very white, sharp teeth. Marie, directed by her father, put a nut into his mouth, and—*knack*—he bit it in two, so that the shells fell down, and Marie got the kernel. Then it was

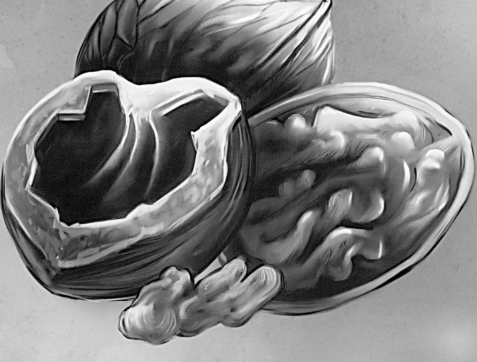

explained to all that this charming little man belonged to the Nutcracker family. "And," said Papa, "as friend Nutcracker seems to have made such an impression on you, Marie, he shall be under your special care, though, as I said, Louise and Fritz are to have the same right to his services as you."

Marie took him into her arms at once, and made him crack some more nuts; but she picked out only the smallest, so that he might not have to open his mouth so terribly wide. Then sister Louise came, and he had to crack some nuts for her too, which duty he seemed very glad to perform, as he kept on smiling.

Fritz was a little tired, so he gave Nutcracker all the biggest and hardest nuts he could find, but all at once there was a *crack-crack*, and three teeth fell out of Nutcracker's mouth, and all his lower jaw was loose and wobbly.

"My poor darling Nutcracker," Marie cried, taking him away from Fritz.

"A nice sort of chap *he* is!" said Fritz. "Calls himself a nutcracker, but can't give a decent bite. Hand him over, Marie!"

"No," said Marie, in tears, "you won't have my darling Nutcracker; see how he's looking at me so mournfully, and showing me his poor sore mouth."

"Nutcracker's as much mine as yours, so hand him over!" said Fritz.

Marie began to cry bitterly, and wrapped the wounded Nutcracker up in her little handkerchief. Papa and Mama came with Drosselmeier, who took Fritz's side. But Papa said, "I have put Nutcracker in Marie's special charge, and as he seems to have need of her care, she has full power over him."

Marie got Nutcracker's lost teeth together, bound a pretty ribbon about his poor chin, and then wrapped the poor little fellow more tenderly and carefully in her handkerchief. She held him, rocking him like a child in her arms, as she looked at the picture books. She grew quite angry with Godpapa Drosselmeier because he laughed and kept asking how she could make such a fuss about an ugly little fellow like that.

She said, "Who knows, Godpapa, if you were dressed the same as my darling Nutcracker, you might look almost as handsome as he does."

Marie did not understand why Papa and Mama laughed so heartily, nor why Godpapa Drosselmeier did not laugh as much as before.

The Battle

It was getting close to midnight before the children could tear themselves away from all these Yuletide fascinations, and Godpapa Drosselmeier had been gone a considerable time. They remained riveted beside the glass cupboard where all the children's Christmas presents were kept, although their mother reminded them several times that it was long after bedtime.

"Yes," said Fritz, "these poor hussars are tired, and awfully anxious to turn in for the night." With that he went off.

But Marie begged for just a little while longer, saying she had such a number of things to see to, and promising that as soon as she had gotten them all settled she would go to bed at once. Marie was a very good child, so her mother allowed her to remain for a little longer with her toys. "Come to bed soon, Marie, or you'll never be up in time in the morning," said her mother as she went away into the bedroom.

As soon as Marie was alone, she laid the Nutcracker softly down on the table, gently unrolled the handkerchief, and examined his wounds. Nutcracker was very pale, but at the same time he was smiling with a melancholy kindliness that went straight to Marie's heart.

"Oh, my darling little Nutcracker!" said she, very softly, "don't you be vexed because brother Fritz has hurt you so. He didn't mean it, and I'll take the greatest care of you till you're quite better and happy again. And your teeth shall be fixed, and your jaw set right; Godpapa Drosselmeier will see to that—"

Marie could not finish what she was going to say, because at the mention of Godpapa Drosselmeier, the Nutcracker made a most horrible, ugly face. This was only for an instant, however, and just as Marie was going to be terribly frightened, she found that she was looking at the very same nice, kindly face that she had seen before. She decided that it was nothing but a draft of air making the lamp flicker that had seemed to produce the change.

"Well!" she said, "I certainly am a silly girl to be so easily frightened and think that a wooden doll could make faces at me!"

She took him in her arms again, approached the cupboard, and knelt down beside it to address another of her dolls, Miss Clara. "I'm going to ask a favor of you, Miss Clara—that you will give up your bed to this poor sick, wounded Nutcracker, and make yourself as comfortable as you can on the sofa here."

Miss Clara looked very grand and disdainful in her Christmas dress, but said nothing.

Marie laid Nutcracker carefully and tenderly on the bed, wrapped a pretty ribbon around his hurt jaw, and drew the covers up to his nose. She moved the bed, with Nutcracker in it, to the upper shelf, so that it was placed safely near Fritz's hussars. She closed the cupboard and was moving away to go to bed when she began to hear rustling and rattling all round—behind the stove, under the chairs, behind the cupboards. Marie looked at the clock on the wall, and saw that the big gilt owl that was on the top of it had drooped its wings so that they covered the whole of the clock. Then the clock rang twelve times.

Marie grew terribly frightened, and was going to rush away, when she noticed that Godpapa Drosselmeier was now up on the top of the clock instead of the owl, with his yellow coattails hanging down on both sides like wings. She called out,

"Godpapa! Why are you up there? Come down and don't frighten me so terribly, you naughty Godpapa Drosselmeier!"

But presently she heard the sound of thousands of little feet behind the walls, and thousands of little glittering eyes began to appear between the cracks of the woodwork. Marie saw that mice were peeping and squeezing themselves out through every crack, forming themselves into ordered lines just as Fritz's soldiers did. Marie was amused by this, until suddenly there came a sharp and terribly shrill noise.

Right at her feet, broken stone came bursting up, and then seven mouse heads, with seven shining crowns upon them, rose through the floor. Quickly the body of the mouse with those seven crowned heads forced its way up through the floor, and the enormous creature shouted to the assembled multitude, squeaking to them with all seven mouths in full chorus. The entire army set itself in motion, and went *trot, trot,* right up to the cupboard—and to Marie, who was standing beside it.

Right behind Marie a movement seemed to commence in the cupboard. Turning, she saw bright light, and dolls and little figures of various kinds were running around. At this point, Nutcracker rose from his bed and sprang with both feet onto the shelf, crying out at the top of his voice as he drew his little sword, "My trusty friends, are you ready to stand by me in this great battle?"

Immediately the toys replied, "Yes, your highness! We will follow you to victory!"

Waving his glittering sword, Nutcracker sprang, like a bird, over the ledge of the cupboard and down to the floor. Under the big table, the hordes of the mouse army had assembled under the command of the terrible mouse with the seven heads.

"Beat the drum!" cried Nutcracker. Immediately the drummer began to roll his drum so that the windows of the glass cupboard rattled and resounded. Then Marie saw the lids of the boxes in which Fritz's army had been stored burst open, and the soldiers all came out and jumped down to the bottom shelf, where they formed up in good order. Nutcracker hurried up and down the ranks, speaking words of encouragement.

Marie heard neighing in the cupboard, and Fritz's cavalry—including the new glittering hussars—marched out on horseback. Next, Fritz's artillery came rattling up, and formed a line in front of the cavalry. Then the cannons went *boom-boom!* and Marie saw sugar-plum cannonballs land among the mice, who were powdered quite white by them. A group of heavy guns on mama's footstool did the greatest damage; and *poom-poom-poom!* kept up a fire of gingerbread nuts into the enemy's ranks, mowing the mice down in great numbers.

The enemy, however, was not slowed. Marie could barely see what was happening, for all the smoke and dust; but every soldier fought with the utmost bravery, and for a long time it was doubtful which side would gain the day. The Mouse King and the mice squeaked and screamed; and Nutcracker's powerful voice was heard shouting words of command and issuing important orders.

During the hottest part of the battle, masses of mouse cavalry had made a most determined advance upon the left wing of Nutcracker's force, uttering loud and horrible squeakings. The unfortunate Nutcracker soon found himself driven back to the front of the cupboard, with a very small remnant of his army.

"Bring up the reserves!" shouted Nutcracker. A small contingent of brown gingerbread men and women advanced, but they were so clumsy that they never hit any of the enemy, and the mice soon bit their legs off so that they tumbled topsy-turvy.

Nutcracker was now in a position of extreme peril. He tried to jump up to the bottom ledge of the cupboard, but his legs were not long enough. At this moment two of the enemy's riflemen seized him by his wooden cloak, and the king of the mice rushed up to him, squeaking in triumph out of all his seven throats.

Marie could contain herself no longer. "Oh, my poor Nutcracker!" she sobbed, taking her left shoe off and throwing it as hard as she could straight at the Mouse King.

Instantly everything vanished and disappeared. All was silence as Marie fainted to the floor.

The Story of the Hard Nut

When Marie awoke she was lying in her little bed. The sun was shining brightly through the window, which was covered with frost-flowers.

"Mother," whispered Marie, "have all those horrid mice gone away, and is Nutcracker quite safe?"

"Don't talk such nonsense, Marie," answered her mother. "You're a very naughty girl, and have caused us all a great deal of anxiety."

"Oh, Mother," said Marie, "there was a tremendous battle between the toys and the mice; and I was terribly frightened that the mice were going to take Nutcracker a prisoner. Then I threw my shoe at the mice, and after that I know nothing more."

"Never mind, dear, keep yourself quiet. The mice are all gone away, and Nutcracker's in the cupboard, quite safe and sound."

Later the door opened and in came Godpapa Drosselmeier, saying, "I've come to see with my own eyes how Marie's getting on."

When Marie saw Godpapa Drosselmeier in his yellow coat, the battle with the mice came back to her so vividly that she couldn't help crying out, "Godpapa Drosselmeier, how nasty you were! I saw you when you were sitting on the clock. Why didn't you help Nutcracker?"

He hastened to sit down beside Marie's bed, and whispered to her, "Don't be upset with me. To make up for it, here's something that I know will please you greatly."

He reached into one of his pockets and slowly brought out Nutcracker, whose broken teeth and jaw he had fixed. Marie shouted for joy.

"But you must admit, Marie," said her godpapa, "that Nutcracker is far from being what you might call a handsome fellow. If you like I'll tell you how it was that he became ugly, and about the Princess Pirlipat, the evil Mouseyrinks, and the clever Clockmaker."

"Go on then—do tell it," cried Marie, and Drosselmeier began his story.

Pirlipat was a princess by birth. The king was quite beside himself with joy over his beautiful little daughter, and he danced round and round, crying, "Did anybody ever see anything so lovely as my little Pirlipat?"

Indeed, there was no denying that a lovelier baby than Princess Pirlipat had never been born. Her little face looked as if it were woven of the most delicate white and rose-colored silk; her eyes were of sparkling azure, and her hair was all in little curls like threads of gold. All was joy and gladness, except that the queen was very anxious and uneasy, and nobody could tell why. She had Pirlipat's cradle guarded not only by guards at the doors of the nursery but also by six nurses all around the room at night, each petting a cat in her lap so that it might never stop purring.

Once upon a time, many great kings and very grand princes had been assembled at Pirlipat's father's court, and the king, to show that he had no lack of gold and silver, made up his mind to give a grand banquet. He said to the queen, "My darling, you know exactly how I like my sausages made!"

The queen undertook the important duty of making the sausages herself. So the queen put on her damask kitchen apron, and soon the most delicious aromas rose steaming out of the kitchen. As the fat for the sausages began to brown, a delicate little whispering voice said, "Give me some of that, sister! I am a queen as well as yourself; give me some."

The queen knew it was Dame Mouseyrinks, who was queen of the realm of Mousolia and lived under the kitchen hearth. The queen was a kindhearted woman, and said, "Come out, then, Dame Mouseyrinks; of course you shall taste my browned fat."

So Dame Mouseyrinks came running out as fast as she could, held up her pretty little paws, and took morsel after morsel of the browned fat as the queen held them out to her. But then all Dame Mouseyrink's uncles, and her cousins, and her aunts, and her seven sons came jumping out too. They all started eating the browned fat, and the queen was too frightened to keep them away. Most fortunately, someone eventually entered and scared the intruders away, so that a little of the browned fat was left for the sausages.

The trumpets summoned all the guests to the feast. With his crown on and his scepter in his hand, the king took his seat at the head of the table. When the sausages were handed round, the king eagerly ate one, then fell back in his seat as if gravely ill, stammering, "Too little fat!"

The queen cried, "Alas! Dame Mouseyrinks, her uncles, her seven sons, her cousins, and her aunts came and ate up nearly all the fat!"

The king jumped up,
all anger, and resolved to take
revenge on Dame Mouseyrinks and her family for
embarrassing him in front of his guests by ruining the sausages.
He summoned the court clockmaker, Drosselmeier, who invented
ingenious little machines into which pieces of browned fat were
inserted; and he placed these machines all around the dwelling of Dame
Mouseyrinks. Enticed by the fragrant odor of the browned fat, all her seven sons,
and a great many of her uncles, her cousins, and her aunts walked into Drosselmeier's little
machines, and were immediately captured.

But Dame Mouseyrinks was too smart to be caught. One day when the queen was cooking,
Dame Mouseyrinks suddenly appeared, and warned, "My sons and my uncles, my cousins and
my aunts are gone. Beware, lady, lest the queen of the mice bites your little princess in two!"

With that she vanished, but the queen was very frightened and took precautions to protect
her little Pirlipat.

One night, just after midnight, one of Pirlipat's nurses woke suddenly from a deep sleep.
Everything lay buried in slumber, not a purr to be heard. Close beside her, the nurse saw
a great, hideous mouse standing on its hind legs, with its horrid head near the princess's face!
She sprang up with a scream of terror. Everybody awoke, but Dame Mouseyrinks (for she was
the great big mouse in Pirlipat's cradle) ran quickly away.

The noise awoke Pirlipat, who cried terribly. But the beautiful, delicate little thing had turned into an enormous bloated head at the top of a diminutive, crumpled-up body. Pale, wooden-looking eyes stared out from where the lovely azure-blue pair had once been, while her mouth now stretched across from the one ear to the other.

The king laid all the blame on the court clockmaker, Drosselmeier. He commanded that Drosselmeier must restore Princess Pirlipat to her pristine condition within four weeks.

As the weeks passed, the little princess kept on cracking nuts, an occupation that seemed to afford her much quiet satisfaction. The clockmaker was struck by Pirlipat's remarkable appetite for nuts and her strong teeth. He took his suspicions about Pirilpat's condition to his friend, the court astrologer, and together they read many books about mysterious subjects and consulted the stars to determine how to proceed. At last, they agreed that to be delivered from the enchantment, the princess must eat the sweet kernel of the nut Crackatook.

This nut Crackatook had a shell so hard that you might have fired a cannon at it without damaging it. Moreover, their research suggested that this nut must be cracked in the princess's presence by the teeth of a young man. This man had to hand the kernel to her with his eyes closed, then make seven steps backwards without a stumble.

After several nice young gentlemen had tried and failed to crack the nut, the king promised that whoever disenchanted the princess would marry his daughter and become prince of the kingdom. The charming, gentle young nephew of Drosselmeier begged to be allowed to make an attempt.

The clockmaker's nephew had appeared the previous Christmas in a beautiful red coat with gold trimmings, a sword by his side, and a fine wig with a pigtail. Thus appareled, he had stood in his father's shop cracking nuts for the young ladies, who called him the handsome nutcracker.

33

None of the previous young
men had pleased the princess so
much. She pressed her little hands to her heart
and sighed, "Ah, I hope it will be he who will crack
the nut, and be my husband."

When he had politely saluted the king, the queen, and Princess
Pirlipat, he received the nut Crackatook, put it between his teeth,
and—*crack-crack*—the shell was shattered into a number of pieces. He
neatly cleared the kernel from the pieces of husk that were sticking to
it, and, bowing, presented it courteously to the princess, after which he

closed his eyes and began
his backward steps. The princess
swallowed the kernel and transformed
back into a wonderfully beautiful lady.

The king and all his court celebrated, as they had done
at Pirlipat's birth. All this tremendous tumult interfered with
young Drosselmeier's seven backward steps. But he collected himself
as best he could, and was just stretching out his right foot to make his
seventh step, when up came Dame Mouseyrinks through the floor so
that young Drosselmeier stepped on her and stumbled.

In an instant he was transformed, just as the princess had been before. His body shriveled up and could scarcely support the great shapeless head, with its enormous, projecting eyes and wide, gaping mouth. In the place where his pigtail had once been, a scanty wooden cloak now hung down, controlling the movements of his lower jaw.

The clockmaker saw that Dame Mouseyrinks had not escaped punishment, for young Drosselmeier had squashed her. But as Dame Mouseyrinks lay in agony, she swore that her seven-headed son would come after the Nutcracker for revenge.

In the meantime no one else had noticed the fate of young Drosselmeier. When the king instructed the young hero to come forward for his reward and his transformation was revealed, the princess cried, "Oh, please take away that horrid Nutcracker!"

The king laid all the blame on the clockmaker, and ordered him to be banished forever.

The court astrologer predicted that young Drosselmeier would yet be a prince and a king; but also that his deformity would only disappear after the seven-headed son of Dame Mouseyrinks should perish by his hand, and a lady should fall in love with him despite his deformity.

As Godpapa Drosselmeier finished his tale, Marie thought the Princess Pirlipat was a nasty, ungrateful thing.

Fritz, on the other hand, was of opinion that if Nutcracker had been a proper sort of fellow, he would soon have fought the Mouse King, and gotten his good looks back again.

Victory

When Marie was quite well again, she immediately checked on her toys in the glass cupboard, which looked very fine indeed—everything new and shiny. Above all, Marie found her dear Nutcracker again, smiling at her on the second shelf with his teeth all fixed. As she looked at this pet of hers with much fondness, it suddenly struck her that Godpapa Drosselmeier's story had been about Nutcracker, who was none other than young Mr. Drosselmeier, Godpapa Drosselmeier's delightful nephew, under the spell of Dame Mouseyrinks. For Marie couldn't doubt for a moment that the clever clockmaker at Pirlipat's father's court was Godpapa Drosselmeier himself.

"But why didn't your uncle help you?" Marie cried, sorrowfully, as she felt more and more clearly every moment that in the battle she had witnessed, the question in dispute had been no less a matter than Nutcracker's crown and kingdom.

While the clever Marie was weighing all these things in her mind, she kept expecting that

Nutcracker and his vassals would give some indications of being alive, and make some movements as she looked at them. Everything in the cupboard, however, kept quite motionless and still. Marie thought this was the effect of Dame Mouseyrinks's enchantments and those of her seven-headed son, which still were keeping up their power.

"But," she said, "though you're not able to move, or to say the least little word to me, dear Mr. Drosselmeier, I know you understand me. You will always have my assistance when you require it."

Nutcracker still kept quiet and motionless. But Marie fancied that a gentle sigh came breathing through the glass cupboard.

Twilight came on. Marie's father came in with Godpapa Drosselmeier, and the family talked in the merriest manner about all sorts of things. Marie had taken her little stool, and sat down at her godpapa's feet.

She looked Drosselmeier full in the face with her great blue eyes, and said,

"I know now, Godpapa, that my Nutcracker is your nephew. The prophecy has come true: he is a king and a prince. But you know as well as I do that he is at war with that horrid king of the mice. Why don't you help him?"

Godpapa smiled strangely and took little Marie on his knee, speaking more gently to her than he had ever been known to do before.

"You are a born princess, Marie dear, like Pirlipat, and reign in a bright beautiful country," he said. "But you still have much to suffer, if you mean to befriend poor transformed Nutcracker; for the king of the mice lies in wait for him at every turn. But I cannot help him; only you can do that. So be faithful and true."

Neither Marie nor any of the others knew what Godpapa Drosselmeier meant by these words.

It was not very long before Marie was awakened one bright moonlit night by a curious noise that came from one of the corners of her room.

"Oh, dear me! Here come these abominable mice again!" cried Marie, as the king of the mice worked himself out through a hole in the wall. At last he came into the room and got onto the little table at her bedside with a great jump.

"Give me your sweets!" he cried. "Out with your candy, marzipan, and iced gingerbread cakes! Don't pause to argue! If yield them you won't, I'll chew up Nutcracker! See if I don't!"

As he cried out these terrible words, he gnashed and chattered his teeth most frightfully, and then made off again through the hole in the wall. Marie was so upset that she scarcely uttered a word the next morning. A hundred times she felt impelled to tell someone what had happened. But she thought, "Of course none of them would believe me. They would only laugh at me."

She knew that to protect Nutcracker she would have to sacrifice all her sweet things; so she laid out all she had at the bottom of the cupboard the next evening.

"I can't make out how the mice have got into the sitting room," said her mother the following morning. "There never were any there before. See, Marie, they've eaten up all your sweets."

And so it was: the Mouse King hadn't found the marzipan altogether to his taste but had gnawed all around the edges of it, so that what he had left of it had to be thrown into the trash. Marie never minded about her sweets, being delighted to think that she had saved Nutcracker with them. But the next night the king of the mice came again, with his eyes glaring worse than the night before.

"Give me your sugar toys," he cried, "Give them you must, or else I'll chew Nutcracker up into dust!"

Then he was gone again.

Marie was very disappointed. Not only had she a charming little shepherd looking after a flock of milk-white sheep, with a nice dog jumping about them, but two postmen with letters in their hands, and four couples of prettily dressed young gentlemen and most beautifully dressed young ladies. Then there were two or three dancers, and back in the corner there was a little baby with red cheeks, and this was Marie's darling. The tears came to her eyes.

"Ah!" she cried, turning to Nutcracker, "I really will do all I can to help you. But it's very hard."

Nutcracker looked at her so pitifully that she determined to sacrifice everything—for she remembered the Mouse King with all his seven mouths wide open to swallow the poor young fellow. So that night she set down all her sugar figures in front of the cupboard, as she had the sweets the night before.

"This is really getting too bad," said Marie's mother the next morning. "Some nasty mouse must have made a hole in the glass cupboard, for poor Marie's sugar figures are all eaten and gnawed." Marie really could not restrain her tears. But she was soon able to smile again, for she thought, "What does it matter? Nutcracker is safe."

In the evening Marie's mother was telling her father and Godpapa Drosselmeier about the mischief that some mouse was doing in the children's cupboard, and her father said, "It's a regular nuisance! What a pity it is that we can't get rid of it. It's destroying all the poor child's things."

"Godpapa Drosselmeier's the man to get us a mousetrap," said Fritz; "it was he who invented them, you know."

How did it fare with Marie that night? The horrible Mouse King came and hissed into Marie's ear, "Hand out your picture books—none of your scornful looks!—or, if you don't, leave you I won't—Nutcracker I'll bite—drag him out of your sight!"

Marie was overwhelmed with sorrow, and was looking quite upset when her

42

mother said to her next morning, "This horrid mouse hasn't been caught. But we'll catch the nasty thing yet, never fear."

As soon as Marie was alone, she went up to the glass cupboard and said to Nutcracker, in a voice broken by sobs, "Ah, my dear Mr. Drosselmeier, what can I do? Even if I give that horrid king of the mice all my picture books, he's sure to go on asking for more. What shall I do?"

As she was crying, she noticed that a great red spot had been left on Nutcracker's neck since the eventful night of the battle. She took him carefully out of his shelf and began to wipe off this red spot with her handkerchief. Soon she found that Nutcracker was growing warmer and warmer in her hand and beginning to move! She put him back into the cupboard as fast as she could. His mouth began to wobble and he began to whisper, with much difficulty, "Ah, dearest Miss Stahlbaum—how deeply I am indebted to you! But don't sacrifice any of your picture books for me. Get me a sword and I'll manage the rest. . . ."

There Nutcracker's speech died away, and his eyes, which had been expressing the most sympathetic grief, grew lifeless again.

Marie jumped for joy, for she now

43

knew how to help Nutcracker. That evening, when their father and mother had gone out, she told Fritz what had passed between her and Nutcracker about the king of the mice, and what she needed to rescue Nutcracker.

Fritz replied, "I placed an old Colonel on retirement yesterday, so that he has no further use for his saber, which is sharp." Fritz fetched the Colonel and removed his saber—still a bright and handsome silver weapon—and secured it about Nutcracker.

The next night Marie could not close an eye for anxiety. About midnight she fancied she heard a commotion in the sitting room, and all at once came a shrill "Squeak!"

"The king of the mice!" she cried, and jumped out of bed. Everything was silent, but soon she heard a gentle tapping at the door of her room, and a soft voice said, "Please open your door, dearest Miss Stahlbaum! Don't be alarmed; good, happy news!"

She opened the door as quickly as possible. There stood Nutcracker, with his sword in his right hand, and a little candle in his left. When he saw Marie he knelt down on one knee, and said, "The treacherous king of the mice lies vanquished! Please accept these tokens of victory."

Nutcracker took from his left arm the seven crowns of the Mouse King and handed them to Marie, who received them with pleasure. Nutcracker rose, and continued, "Miss Stahlbaum, if you would follow me for a few steps, what glorious and beautiful things I could show you. Do come with me, dearest lady!"

Toyland

Marie did not hesitate for a moment to go with good, kind Nutcracker. "I will go with you, dear Mr. Drosselmeier, but it mustn't be very far, because I haven't had any sleep yet."

"Then we will go by the shortest route," said Nutcracker, "although it is, perhaps, the most difficult."

He went in front, followed by Marie, till he stopped before the big old wardrobe. Marie was surprised to see its doors wide open, so that she could see her father's fox-fur traveling cloak hanging in the front. Nutcracker scrambled up the cloak, reaching for the big tassel that was fastened at the back of it by a thick cord. He gave this tassel a tug, and a pretty little ladder of cedar-wood let itself quickly down through one of the armholes of the cloak.

"Now, Miss Stahlbaum, step up that ladder, if you will be so kind," said Nutcracker. Marie did so. But as soon as she had got up through the armhole and begun to look out at the neck, all at once a dazzling

45

light shimmered over her, and she found herself standing on a lovely, sweet-scented meadow, from which millions of sparks were streaming upward, like the glitter of beautiful gems.

"This is Candy Meadow, where we are now," said Nutcracker. "But we'll go in at that gate there."

Marie looked up and saw a beautiful gateway on the meadow, only a few steps away. It seemed to be made of white, brown, and raisin-colored marble; but when she came close to it she saw it was all baked sugar-almonds and raisins, which—as Nutcracker explained when they were going through it—was the reason it was called "Almond and Raisin Gate." There was a balcony running around the upper part of it, apparently made of caramel, and in this balcony six monkeys, dressed in red doublets, were playing brass instruments. It was all that Marie could do to notice that she was walking along on a beautiful variegated marble pavement that was really a mosaic of lozenges of all colors.

Presently the sweetest of odors came breathing round her, streaming from a beautiful little wood on both sides of the way. There was such a glittering and sparkling among the dark foliage that one could see all the gold and silver fruits hanging on the many-tinted stems, and these stems and branches were all ornamented and dressed up in ribbons and bunches

of flowers,
like brides and
bridegrooms, and
festive wedding guests.
The gold leaf and tinsel
rustled and tinkled like beautiful
music, to which the sparkling lights danced.

"Oh, how charming this is!" cried Marie, enraptured.

"This is Christmas Wood, dearest Miss Stahlbaum," said Nutcracker.

"Ah!" said Marie, "if I could only stay here for a while! Oh, it is so lovely!"

Nutcracker clapped his hands, and immediately a number of little shepherds and
shepherdesses and hunters and huntresses appeared, so white and delicate that you would have
thought they were made of pure sugar. They brought a beautiful gold chair, laid a white satin
cushion in it, and politely invited Marie to take a seat. As soon as she did so, the shepherds and
shepherdesses danced a pretty ballet, to which the hunters and huntresses played the music on
their horns, and then they all disappeared among the thickets.

"These people belong to our Wire Ballet Troupe, and can only do the same dance over and over again," said Nutcracker. "Shall we go on a little farther?"

"Oh, I enjoyed it immensely!" said Marie, as she stood up and followed Nutcracker, who led the way. They walked along a gently rippling brook that seemed to be the source of all the perfume that filled the wood.

"This is Orange Brook," said Nutcracker. "Except for its sweet scent, it is not as fine a water as the River Lemonade, a beautiful broad stream that falls—as this one does also—into the Almond Milk Sea."

Indeed, Marie soon heard a louder splashing and rushing, and came in sight of the River Lemonade, which went rolling along in swelling waves of a yellowish color between banks covered with plants and shrubs that shone like green jewels. A remarkable freshness and coolness exhaled from this fine river. Not far from it, a dark yellow stream crept sluggishly along, giving out a most delicious odor; and on its banks sat numbers of pretty children, angling for fat little fishes, which they ate as soon as they caught them.

A short distance farther, on the banks of this stream, stood a nice little village. The houses of this village, and the church, the barns, and so forth, were all dark brown with gold roofs, and many of the walls looked as if they were plastered over with lemon peel and shelled almonds.

"That is Gingerthorpe on the Honey River," said Nutcracker. "It is famed for the good looks of its inhabitants; but they are very short-tempered people, because they suffer so much from toothache. So we won't go there at present."

At this moment Marie caught sight of a little town where the houses were all sorts of colors and quite transparent. Nutcracker went on toward this town, and Marie heard a noise of bustle and merriment and saw nice little folks unloading a number of wagons that were pulled up in the marketplace. What they were unloading from the wagons looked like packages of colored paper and tablets of chocolate.

"This is Bonbonville," Nutcracker said. "A delegation has just arrived from Paperland and the King of Chocolate. These poor Bonbonville people have been threatened lately by the Fly Admiral's forces, so they are covering their houses over with their presents from Paperland and constructing fortifications with the fine pieces of workmanship the Chocolate King has sent them. But we are not going to restrict ourselves to seeing the small towns and villages of this country. Let us be off to the metropolis."

He stepped quickly onward, and Marie followed him. Soon a beautiful rosy vapor began to rise from a red, shining water, which went splashing and rushing away in front of them in wavelets. On this delightful water, which kept broadening out wider and wider like a great lake, the loveliest swans were floating, white as silver with collars of gold. They were singing the most beautiful songs, at which little fish, glittering like diamonds, danced up and down in the rosy ripples.

"Oh!" cried Marie, in the greatest delight, "this must be the lake Godpapa Drosselmeier was once going to make for me, and I am the girl who is to play with the swans."

Nutcracker laughed, and said, "My uncle could never make a thing of this kind. But don't let us bother about that. Rather let us go sailing over Lake Rosa to the metropolis."

The Metropolis

Nutcracker clapped his little hands again, and the waves of Lake Rosa began to splash higher. Marie became aware of a sort of car approaching from the distance, made of glittering precious stones of every color and drawn by two dolphins with scales of gold. Marie and Nutcracker gently stepped into the car, which immediately began to move over the lake of its own accord. The two golden-scaled dolphins lifted their nostrils and sent streams of crystal high in the air; and as these fell down in glittering, sparkling rainbows, Marie heard the sound of two delicate, silvery voices, singing.

Marie looked into the perfumed rosy waves and saw a pretty girl's face smiling back at her. "Oh, look at Princess Pirlipat," she cried, clapping her hands with gladness, "smiling at me so charmingly down there!"

But Nutcracker said, "That is not Princess Pirlipat, dearest Miss Stahlbaum, it is only your own lovely face smiling up from the rosy waves."

Marie was terribly embarrassed, but just then the car arrived at its destination. Marie found herself in a small grove, almost more beautiful even than Christmas Wood, everything glittered and sparkled so in it. The fruit on the trees was not only of very curious colors but also had the most delicious perfume.

"Ah!" said Nutcracker, "here we are in Sugar Almond Grove, and yonder lies the metropolis."

Marie took in the full splendor and magnificence of the city that lay stretched out before her on a flowery plain. Not only did the walls and towers shine in the brightest and most gorgeous colors, but the shapes and appearance of the buildings were like nothing to be seen on earth. Instead of roofs the houses had beautiful twining crowns, and the towers were garlanded with beautiful leaf work carved into exquisite, intricate designs. As they passed through the gateway, which was made entirely of macaroons and sugared fruits, silver soldiers presented arms, and a little man in a brocade robe threw himself on Nutcracker's neck, crying, "Welcome, dearest prince! Welcome to Sweetsburgh!"

Marie was surprised to see such a very grand person recognize young Mr. Drosselmeier as a prince. But she heard such a number of voices making such a laughing and chattering, and such a singing and playing, that she couldn't give her attention to anything else. She asked young Drosselmeier what was the meaning of it all.

"Oh, it is nothing unusual, dearest Miss Stahlbaum," he answered. "Sweetsburgh is a large, populous city, full of merriment and entertainment. Come on a little farther."

After a few paces more they were in the great marketplace, which presented the most magnificent appearance. All the houses around it were made of filigreed sugar, with balconies towering above

balconies; and in the center stood a lofty cake covered with sugar, with fountains around it spouting orangeade, lemonade, and other delicious beverages into the air. The channels at the sides of the sidewalks were full of creams. But prettier than all this were the delightful little people who were crowding around by the thousands, producing all that jubilant uproar that Marie had heard from the distance. There were beautifully dressed ladies and gentlemen, officers and soldiers, clergymen, shepherds, jesters—in short, people of every conceivable kind to be found in the world.

Marie now found herself before a castle with a hundred

beautiful towers. On its walls were
rich bouquets of violets, narcissus,
tulips, and carnations, whose deep, glowing
colors accented the dazzling whiteness of the walls.
The great dome of the central building and the pyramid-
shaped roofs of the towers were covered with thousands of sparkling
gold and silver stars.

"Aha!" said Nutcracker, "here we are at Marzipan Castle at last!"
Marie was in awe of this magic palace, but it did not escape her
notice that the roof was missing one of the principal towers, and
that little men up on a scaffold made of cinnamon sticks were busy
putting it on again. Before she had had time to ask Nutcracker about
this, he said, "This beautiful castle was recently threatened with
total destruction. Sweet-tooth the giant happened to be passing
by, and he bit off the top of that tower there and was beginning
to gnaw at the great dome. But the Sweetsburgh people brought
him a whole quarter of the town as tribute, and a considerable
slice of Sugar Almond Grove as well. This satisfied his
mouth, and he went on his way."

At this moment soft, beautiful music was heard, and out
came twelve little pages with clove-stick torches. Each of
their heads was a pearl, their bodies were emeralds and
rubies, and their feet were pure gold. After them came

57

four ladies about the size of Marie's Miss Clara, but so gloriously and brilliantly attired that Marie saw in a moment that they must be princesses. They embraced Nutcracker most tenderly and shed tears of gladness, saying, "Oh, dearest prince! Beloved brother!"

Nutcracker wiped away his tears, and then he took Marie by the hand and said, "This is Miss Marie Stahlbaum, the preserver of my life. Had she not thrown her slipper just in the nick of time and procured me the retired Colonel's sword, I would have been bitten to death by the king of the mice. The ladies cried, "Ah! Noble preserver of our beloved royal brother! Excellent Miss Stahlbaum!"

They now conducted Marie and Nutcracker into the castle, to a hall whose walls were composed of sparkling crystal. The princesses made Marie and Nutcracker sit down, and said that they would prepare a banquet. So they went and brought little cups and dishes of the finest Japanese porcelain, and spoons, knives, and forks, and kitchen utensils of gold and silver. Then they fetched the most delightful fruits and sugar things—such as Marie had never seen the like of—and began to squeeze the fruit in the daintiest way with their little hands, and to grate the spices and rub down the sugar-almonds. The prettiest of Nutcracker's sisters handed her a little silver mortar, saying, "Sweet friend, would you mind pounding a little of this sugar-candy?"

As Marie pounded in the mortar with the utmost enjoyment, Nutcracker began to relate all that had happened during the terrible fight between his forces and the army of the king of the mice. It seemed to Marie as if what Nutcracker was saying kept going farther and farther away. Presently she saw a silver mistiness rising up all around, like clouds in which the princesses, Nutcracker, and she herself were floating. And a curious buzzing and humming began, that seemed to die away in the distance; and then she seemed to be going up—up—up, as if on waves constantly rising and swelling higher and higher, higher and higher, higher and higher.

And then came a *prr-poof*, and Marie fell down
from some height.

That was a crash and a tumble! Marie opened
her eyes, and there she was in her own bed. It was
broad daylight, and her mother was standing at
her bedside, saying, "Well, what a sleep you
have had! Breakfast has been ready for
ever so long."

"Oh, mother darling,"
said Marie, "what a
number of places
young Mr.
Drosselmeier has
taken me to in the
night, and what
beautiful things I
have seen!"

Her mother
listened and, when
she had finished, said, "You
have had a long, beautiful dream,
Marie. But now you must put it all out
of your head."

Marie firmly maintained that she had
not been dreaming at all; so her mother took
her to the glass cupboard, lifted out Nutcracker
from his usual position on the second shelf, and said, "You silly
girl, how can you believe that this wooden figure can have life and motion?"

"Ah, mother," answered Marie, "I know perfectly well that Nutcracker is young
Mr. Drosselmeier, Godpapa Drosselmeier's nephew."

Her father and mother both laughed.

60

Marie ran into the next room, took the Mouse King's seven crowns from her little box, and handed them to her mother, saying, "Look, dear mother, these are the Mouse King's seven crowns, which young Mr. Drosselmeier gave me last night as proof that he had won the victory."

Her mother gazed in amazement at the little crowns, which were made of some very brilliant, wholly unknown metal, and both parents urged Marie to tell them where she had really gotten them. But she could only repeat what she had said before. When her father scolded her, she began to cry bitterly, and said, "What can I tell you except the truth?"

At this moment the door opened and Godpapa Drosselmeier came in, crying, "Hello! What's all this? My little Marie crying? What's all this?"

Dr. Stahlbaum told him all about it, and showed him the crowns. As soon as he saw them, he cried out, "Nonsense! These are the crowns I used to wear on my watch chain. I gave them as a present to Marie on her second birthday. Do you mean to tell me you don't remember?"

None of them did remember anything of the kind. Marie ran up to her godpapa, crying, "You know everything, Godpapa Drosselmeier. Tell them. Let them know that my Nutcracker is your nephew, and that it was he who gave me the crowns."

But Drosselmeier made a very angry face, and muttered, "Nonsense!"

Marie's father said, "Marie, let there be an end to all this absurd nonsense. If I ever hear you say again that Nutcracker is your godpapa's nephew, I shall toss not only Nutcracker, but all your other playthings out of the window."

Conclusion

Marie did not dare to say anything more of her adventures. But the memories of that fairy realm haunted her, and the music of that delightful, happy country still rang sweetly in her ears for many years to come. Whenever she allowed her thoughts to dwell on all those glories, she saw them again. Instead of playing as she used to do, she sat quiet and meditative, absorbed within herself.

One day, many years later, Godpapa Drosselmeier was repairing one of the clocks in the house, and Marie was sitting beside the glass cupboard, sunk in her dreams and gazing at Nutcracker. All at once she said, "Dear Mr. Drosselmeier, if you really were alive, I shouldn't be like Princess Pirlipat and despise you because you gave up being a handsome gentleman for my sake!"

"Nonsense!" cried Godpapa Drosselmeier. But as he spoke, there came such a tremendous bang and shock that Marie fell from her chair and fainted.

When she came back to her senses, her mother said, "How could you go and tumble off your chair in that way, a young woman like you? Here is Godpapa Drosselmeier's nephew come to visit. See how good you can be."

Marie looked up. Her godpapa had put on his yellow coat and his white wig, and was smiling. Beside him stood a very handsome young gentleman. He had on a beautiful red coat trimmed with gold lace, white silk stockings, and shoes, with a lovely bouquet of flowers in his shirt frill. The little sword at his side seemed to be made entirely of jewels, it sparkled and shone so, and the little hat under his arm was woven of flocks of silk. He had brought Marie the most delightful toys, including many of the very same figures the Mouse King had eaten up, as well as a beautiful saber for Fritz. He cracked nuts at table for the whole party; the very hardest did not withstand him. He placed them in his mouth with his left hand, tugged at his pigtail with his right, and *crack*! they fell in pieces.

Marie grew rcd as a rose at the sight of this charming young gentleman; and she grew redder still when, after dinner, young Drosselmeier asked her to go with him to the glass cupboard in the sitting room.

As soon as young Drosselmeier was alone with Marie, he went down on one knee and said, "My dearly beloved Miss Stahlbaum! See here at your feet the fortunate Drosselmeier, whose life you saved on this very spot. You were kind enough to say that you would not have despised me, as Princess Pirlipat did, if I had been turned ugly for your sake. Immediately I ceased to be a contemptible Nutcracker, and resumed my former form. Please bless me with your precious hand; share with me my crown and kingdom, and reign with me in Marzipan Castle, for there I now am king."

Marie said gently, "Dear Mr. Drosselmeier, you are a kind gentleman; and as you reign over a delightful country of charming, funny, pretty people, I accept your hand."

So then they were formally
betrothed; and when a year and a
day had come and gone, they say
he came and fetched her away in
a golden coach, drawn by silver
horses. At the marriage there
danced two-and-twenty thousand
of the most beautiful dolls and
other figures, all glittering in
pearls and diamonds.

To this day, Marie is the queen of a realm where all kinds of sparkling Christmas Woods and transparent Marzipan Castles—in short, the most wonderful and beautiful things of every kind—are to be seen, by those who have the eyes to see them.

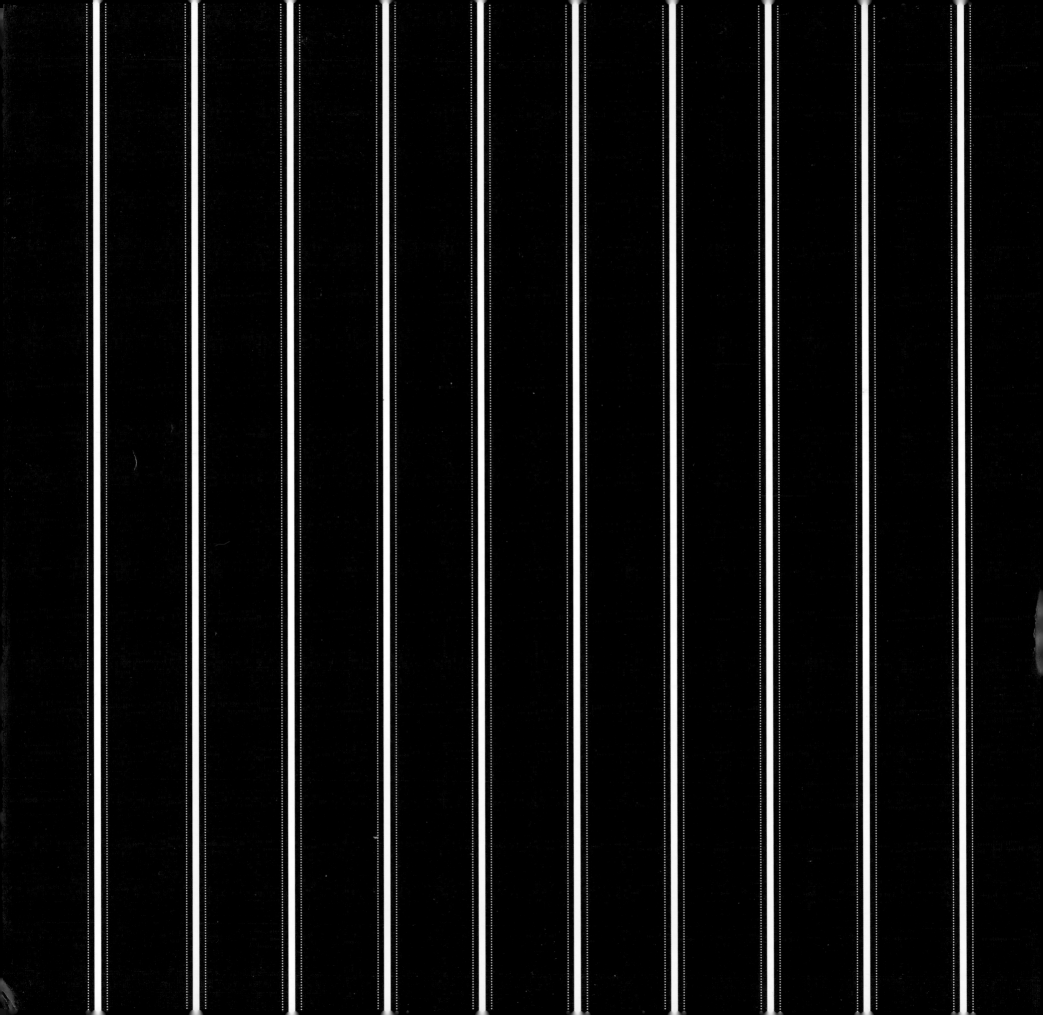